COOL GRINDS

CONTENTS

BY JILLIAN SULLIVAN

ILLUSTRATED BY RAYMOND MCGRATH

PART ONE

> **PREDICT**
> Analyse the cover design and illustration and make a prediction about the target audience.

SOMETIMES...

after a storm, the railway line out of our town has to go through fields of water. If I have to go to the dentist, I always hope they'll close the track. But not today. At long last I have enough money to buy a new skateboard deck and I'm off to the next town to buy it.

I've got enough for any board design I choose. And the best thing is, I didn't have to ask for approval. **I EARNED THE MONEY MYSELF – MOSTLY PUSHING TROLLEYS.**

In our town, you can bet that, with a holiday coming, everyone decides to go to the supermarket at once. I'm out there finding trolleys behind cars and up the next-door alley, as well as in the trolley bays.

> **VISUAL FEATURES**
> How do the visual images and design reflect the world of the skateboarder? What connections can you make?

LANGUAGE FEATURES

Simile/Metaphor/ Personification

What literary devices has the author used here? What was her purpose for using these devices? Is there an underlying message here?

Yesterday after school was my record. I had ten trolleys in a row. It was before the storm and the air was so hot, the tar was almost melting. The trolleys made a long wriggling line and as I pushed them the windscreens of the cars flashed hot sun at me.

We're not allowed to wear sunglasses at work.

THE AIR WAS **SO HOT,** THE TAR WAS ALMOST MELTING

CLARIFY
ollie
360 flip
cool grinds

HEY, JOSH,
YOU DID SOME
COOL GRINDS
ON THE RAIL TODAY

SYMBOLISM

Why has the author introduced a reference to puddles being filled with blue sky? Is this symbolic? What connections can you make to the underlying message?

LANGUAGE FEATURES

Jargon – words and phrases used by a particular group or culture that are often not understood by other people. Find some examples of jargon on this page.

Every hour I worked, and every trolley I pushed, I thought about my skateboard and how I was going to ollie down the five-stair with my new deck.

Last week I nearly did it. Then I hit the ground wrong on my old deck and finally snapped it.

At home, my new stepdad – Raymond – always says to Mum what a waste of time and money skateboarding is. **HE'S NEVER COME TO WATCH ME SKATEBOARD.**

If he did, he'd see how much you have to practise if you want to land any tricks.

He could see the older guys and how fast they go, rolling down the ramp and busting out a 360 flip over the pyramid and landing it.

He might even say to me, "Hey, Josh, you did some cool grinds on the rail today."

Mum comes down and watches me at the park sometimes and she always gets nervous.

"It's all that concrete," she says.

She watches and watches while I mess up my landings, then she turns away just when I do a good one.

I'll bet with my new deck I'll be able to land the five-stair. That's my next project.

INFERENCE

What can you infer about how Raymond's dismissal of skateboarding affects Josh?

After I've bought my deck and fitted it to my trucks and wheels, I'll get a burger, then I'm off to the skatepark. It should be dry. It hasn't rained again, and everywhere I look the puddles are filled up with blue sky.

THE BELLS RING...

as we come through a road crossing. A whole bunch of black and white calves at the fence suddenly run off, as if they've never seen a train before.

In the next field, a red tractor makes a mud trail across the grass. Now I can see a boy in the backyard of a farmhouse, hanging out shirts. The house has a concrete driveway and a ramp up to the door – good enough to skate.

I'm on this train a lot, and sometimes I wonder about all the places I look into.

I WONDER WHAT IT WOULD BE LIKE TO LIVE IN THEM AND HAVE ONE OF THOSE FARMERS, SAY, FOR A DAD, INSTEAD OF RAYMOND.

Last night at the table, when I asked if I could buy my new board today, that was right when the storm broke.

Outside it was thunder and rain falling on the roof so hard it was like we were under a waterfall. And, inside, it was Raymond going on at me about skateboarding – on and on, like the rain.

I just thought of how our town looked as if it was cut off by water some days – as if trying to reach it was hopeless – and yet the train would always get through.

And that's how it is, because here I am, and the guard is calling out the next stop.

The train lets out a blast and I pick up my backpack and check everything's there – my wheels, my skate trucks, my hardware and my skate tool.

I jump out onto the platform and I'm thinking about that five-stair – how I'm going to ollie off that top step, my legs crouched and my new deck flying, then the thud as I land it and roll away.

LANGUAGE FEATURE

Analogy

What analogy did the author use here? How did it help your understanding? What did the author want to convey to the reader?

AND ROLL
AWAY

SETTING

"The house has a concrete driveway and a ramp up to the door – good enough to skate."

What can you infer from this text about how Josh sees his environment?

ONE CHANCE

PART TWO

CLARIFY
sponsored

DOWN AT THE SKATEPARK...

the stands have all been bolted together for tomorrow's competition.

I STAND THERE WITH MY BOARD AND THINK ABOUT THEM FILLED WITH PEOPLE, ALL OF THEM WATCHING ME.

No, better not to think of that. I roll out into the centre of the park. The last car door slams on the last young kid with her blades and the car drives away.

I HAVE THE WHOLE WIDE STRETCH OF CONCRETE TO MYSELF.

The sun is gone from the skatepark now, but above me a white plane is high enough to catch it. It flies bright in the pale sky, lit up like a star.

READING BETWEEN THE LINES

Why do you think the author wrote about, "a white plane is high enough to catch it. It flies bright in the pale sky, lit up like a star"? Is there a parallel or underlying idea suggested in this reference? Give reasons for your answer.

Tomorrow is my first competition. I push off on my board, ollie over the steps, land and speed up for a front-side board slide on the bar. If I can just do it like that when I'm in front of everyone. Do it with style, that's what I want. And one day I might get sponsored and be on a team. Tomorrow is a chance to show what I can do.

I told my stepdad Raymond about the competition. I thought he might come and watch me tomorrow, just for once, but he said he was busy. He had to work.

Mum said she would come, but then I thought about her record. Had she ever seen me land something? Once I fell and busted my board in front of her, and once I busted my finger.

"ALL THAT CONCRETE, MUM. AND I'LL BE GOING FAST."

"I'll shut my eyes and just listen," she said, sorting it, and I grinned back at her.

INFERENCE

What can you infer about the relationship between Josh and his mum?

There are only twenty minutes left till it's dark and I have to catch the train. My wheels whirr across the concrete. I pop a good ollie and skate up the ramp.

IN MY HEAD, I PICTURE EACH TRICK AND THE WAY I WILL LAND IT.

My friend Sam was here earlier, but I had to work. He'll be here to watch me tomorrow, but he doesn't want to enter.

"It's no different doing tricks in front of a stand or just in front of other skaters," I tried telling him. I glance up at the stands again. Tomorrow they'll be crammed with people. The hotdog van will be there. Music will be thumping out, even a DJ. The speakers will blast out the names of the competitors.

MY HEART STARTS THUDDING, EVEN THOUGH I'M HERE ALONE

CLARIFY
wince
kick flip
pop shove-it

At the thought of the crowd, I suddenly feel sick. My heart starts thudding, even though I'm here alone. **LISTEN TO YOUR OWN ADVICE, I THINK.**

I push off on my board, feel the balance in my heels and jump. The board twists in the air. I land too fast and fall backwards. Three times I try to pull off my newest trick – the hard flip. Three times I fall.

In the pines by the park, the starlings are cheeping and cheeping, all excited about twilight, but I want the day to last longer. All afternoon I was filling shelves, wheeling cartons of cans, biscuits and washing powder and lining up trolleys, just waiting to get out here and skate. I wince as I bend down to pick up my board – a few new bruises to add to the old ones.

Time to go. I do a kick flip instead. Then a pop shove-it. Perfect.

I HEAD FOR THE TRAIN, HOPING FOR THE BEST TOMORROW.

BEYOND THE TEXT
What connections can you make to Josh's feelings of sickness when he thinks of performing in front of the crowd?

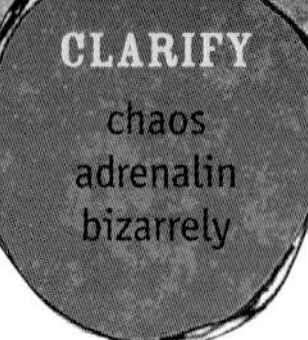

THE LOUD BEAT OF THE MUSIC WEAVES OVER EVERYONE AND REVS UP MY NERVES. THE STANDS ARE FILLING WITH PEOPLE. I CAN'T SEE MUM YET. SAM GLIDES IN AMONG THE OTHER SKATERS ON HIS BOARD. HE DOESN'T HAVE TO THINK ABOUT RIDING OUT ALONE IN FRONT OF EVERYONE.

THE DAY...

of the competition is hot. The grass looks as dry as my throat and the concrete glares in the heat. Sam is waiting by the hotdog van.

WE GO UP THE RAMP TO DROP IN.

The park is crammed with skaters. There are little kids who can hardly stay on their boards. There are guys with bare chests who skim past and bust out tricks and land them. I watch this one guy crouched low over his board – he pops up over the pyramid and lands it.

Sam drops down the ramp into the chaos of skaters. I follow him down, try an ollie, land it and just miss colliding with another guy.

The loud beat of the music weaves over everyone and revs up my nerves. The stands are filling with people. I can't see Mum yet. Sam glides in among the other skaters on his board. He doesn't have to think about riding out alone in front of everyone.

I do an ollie, land it; a kick flip, land it. Still, adrenalin spins and loops through my body on wheels of its own. Bizarrely, my knees start to shake.

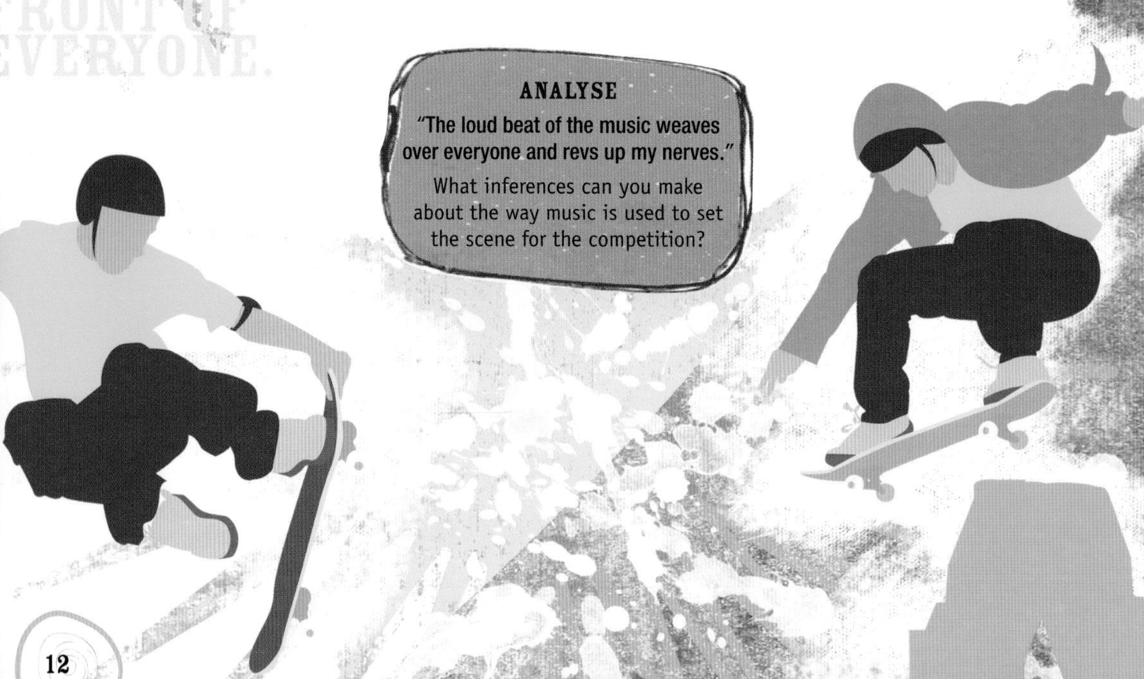

SETTING

Is the author's description of the mood and atmosphere surrounding the competition effective? Why/why not?

LANGUAGE FEATURE

Simile/Metaphor/ Personification

What literary device has the author used here? What was her purpose for using this device? How did it help your understanding of Josh's pre-contest nerves?

ADRENALIN SPINS AND LOOPS THROUGH MY BODY ON WHEELS OF ITS OWN

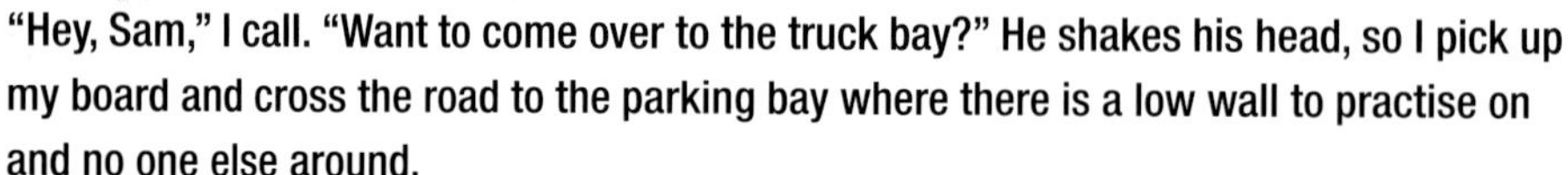

"Hey, Sam," I call. "Want to come over to the truck bay?" He shakes his head, so I pick up my board and cross the road to the parking bay where there is a low wall to practise on and no one else around.

I ride fast towards it, ollie up, nose-grind along it and jump backwards to land. **THE BOARD SHOOTS OUT FROM UNDER ME AND I CRASH TO THE GROUND. I GET UP, RUN AFTER THE BOARD AND HEAD FOR THE WALL AGAIN.**

SAME THING – OLLIE, GRIND, JUMP, CRASH.

CLARIFY
nose-grind

OPINION
Do you think not having pre-contest family support affects Josh? Why/why not?

My board has escaped to the far end of the truck bay and I walk down to get it in case a truck chooses that moment to drive in and end the life of my new deck.

Some days, when I skate, I can land just about everything I do. Those days I push myself. That's how I learned to drop in down the ramp. It's all about confidence, and perseverance.

OTHER DAYS – I DON'T KNOW WHAT IT IS – YOU THINK IT'S GOING TO BE A GOOD DAY, UNTIL YOU END UP BANG ON YOUR HIP AFTER AN EVERYDAY NOSE-GRIND.

And what of today? I look across at the crowded skatepark and my stomach is full of riders swooping and crashing in the bowl.

I think about that five-stair again – how I watched Sam pull it off last week. How he just stomped it. And how I rode at it over and over – that brief airborne hope and then the thud of the concrete. Hip, knee, elbow. Over and over.

I'm not good enough. That's what it comes down to. How did I even think I could be in a competition?

I sit on the wall instead, with my board at my feet. And that's where Sam finds me, just staring at the container in the loading bay.

QUESTION

What is meant by the term **"brief airborne hope"**? What connections can you make to this term?

CHARACTER ANALYSIS

How do you think Josh will resolve his conflict of feelings about the contest? Use factual and inferential information about his character to support your opinion.

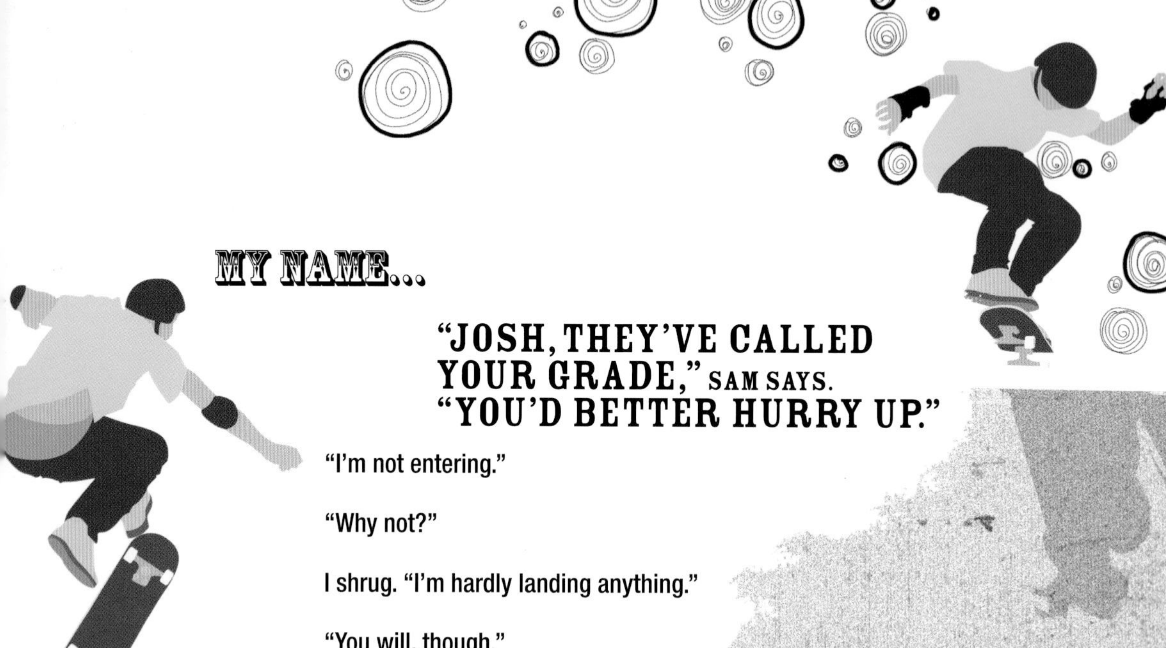

MY NAME...

"JOSH, THEY'VE CALLED YOUR GRADE," SAM SAYS. **"YOU'D BETTER HURRY UP."**

"I'm not entering."

"Why not?"

I shrug. "I'm hardly landing anything."

"You will, though."

"Nah. Doesn't matter."

A kid from our school – Marcus – is up. We sit in the front row and watch him, our boards at our feet. Marcus ollies to flat over the pyramid and lands it. Then he misses a kick flip. He grins at the crowd and runs after his board.

What would it feel like to be out there? My foot bounces up and down on my board as I watch him. It's like that feeling when you're in class and you know the answer, but you don't put your hand up. Or when you have the chance to do something good for someone, and you just sit there instead.

Once, on the train, this young guy had his iPod up loud. I didn't really notice it. A lady stood up and started yelling at him. Then an old guy, really big, stood over him and said, "Turn it off! We don't want that racket inflicted on us."

I thought the two of them were making a worse noise. Also, their bulging eyes and tight, angry faces didn't look good. I wanted to say, "He's just sitting there, but you two are ganging up like bullies."

I didn't say anything, though. I turned and looked out the window. Afterwards I kept hearing their loud, complaining voices and I knew there wasn't another ending, **BECAUSE I DIDN'T TRY TO MAKE ONE.**

In dreams, you can stop and rewind and make them turn out how you want, but in life you just get one chance to do what you can and it's over.

AUTHOR PURPOSE

Why do you think the author introduced the incident on the train at this point? What connections can you make to this incident?

LANGUAGE FEATURE

Analogy

What analogy did the author use? How did it help you understand Josh's thoughts about the contest? What underlying message is the author trying to convey to the reader about those thoughts?

WHEN YOU HAVE THE CHANCE TO DO SOMETHING GOOD FOR SOMEONE AND YOU JUST SIT THERE INSTEAD

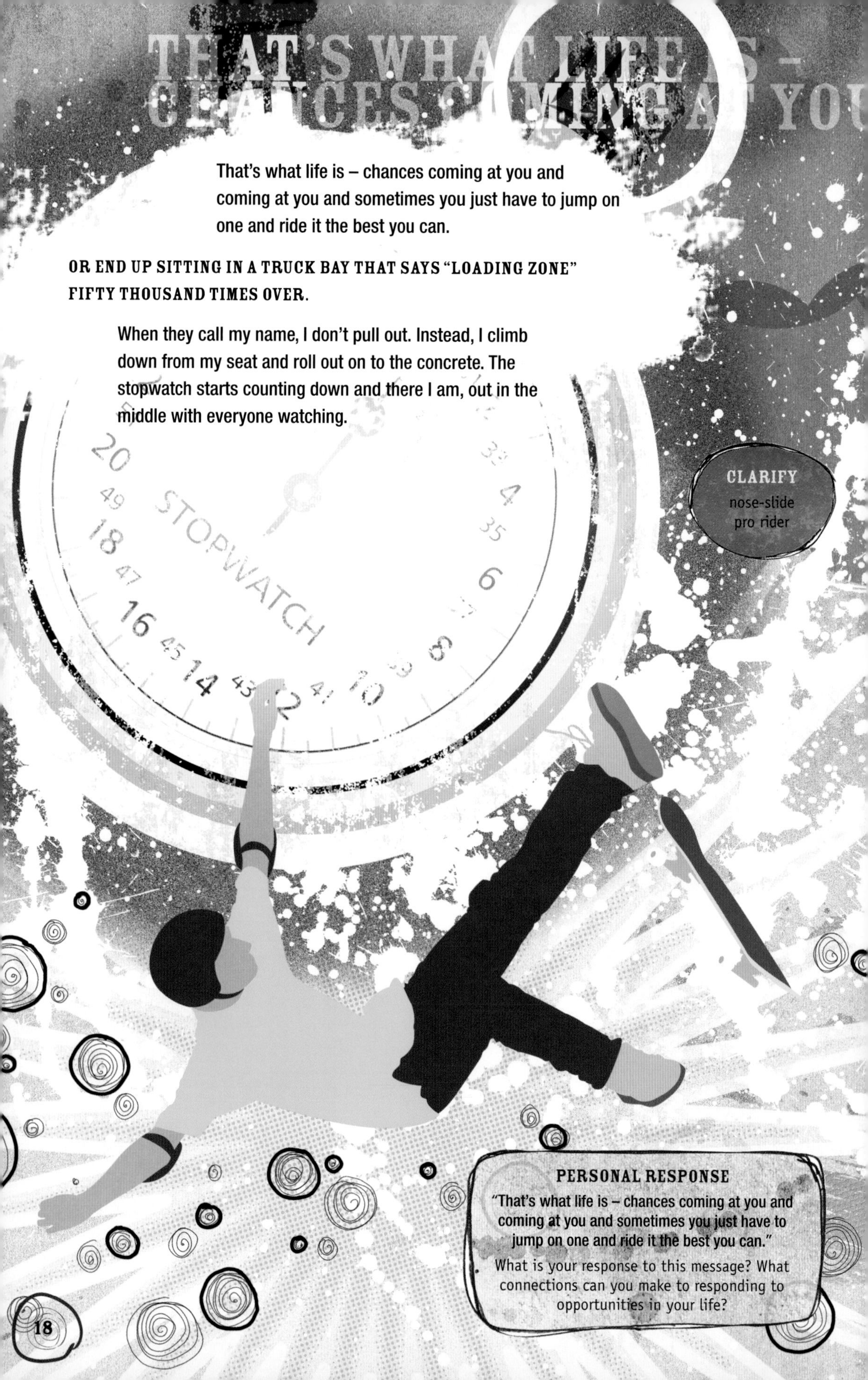

THAT'S WHAT LIFE IS – CHANCES COMING AT YOU

That's what life is – chances coming at you and coming at you and sometimes you just have to jump on one and ride it the best you can.

OR END UP SITTING IN A TRUCK BAY THAT SAYS "LOADING ZONE" FIFTY THOUSAND TIMES OVER.

When they call my name, I don't pull out. Instead, I climb down from my seat and roll out on to the concrete. The stopwatch starts counting down and there I am, out in the middle with everyone watching.

CLARIFY

nose-slide
pro rider

PERSONAL RESPONSE

"That's what life is – chances coming at you and coming at you and sometimes you just have to jump on one and ride it the best you can."

What is your response to this message? What connections can you make to responding to opportunities in your life?

D COMING AT YOU AND SOMETIMES YOU JUST HAVE JUMP ON ONE AND RIDE IT THE BEST YOU CAN

I start off easy – pop a few ollies, nose-slide the ledge. Then I try kick-flipping down the three-stair. The board slips out from under me and I fall on my back. My board races off. I can feel the judges watching me as I walk after it. Three minutes is a long time out in front of a crowd.

One minute to go and I still haven't landed anything good. What about the hard flip? Would trying and failing make it worse?

I roll towards the stands. Thirty seconds to go. This is it. I crouch and stomp my back foot down. The board lifts, flips, rolls over and I catch it and land it cleanly between my feet.

Marcus wins the new trucks and wheels for our grade. A kid I don't know comes second and I line up for third to win a cap.

One of the judges is Darren Sanders, a pro rider. He shakes my hand.

"You landed that hard flip pretty good," he says. "I'll look out for you at the next competition."

I PUT THE CAP ON MY HEAD AND GRIN.

OPINION

Do you think Josh should have tried the hard flip and risked failure in front of the crowd? Why/why not?

GETTING THERE

PART THREE

MUM HOLDS UP A PLATE...

"More potatoes, Josh?" I take two more. It's my stepdad's birthday, though why we have to have a big lunch in the middle of a good skating day, I don't know.

I look across the table and check out the window to make sure the sun is still shining and the weather fine enough to skate.

"It's not Christmas," I'd said to Mum earlier.

She was taking the roast out and putting it on the table.

"Raymond doesn't have a fuss made of him much ever," she said. "So we're going to. We're his family now."

CLARIFY
taking us for granted

"I'M NOT HIS FAMILY," I SAID.

"Yes, you are. We live together."

"Not because I want to. And I'll bet he doesn't want to, either. I just came with the deal."

Mum had passed me the plates. "If we act like a family and live like a family, we will be a family. Just try."

And now lunch for the three of us has gone on for ages. I look at Raymond smiling across at my mother.

"Can I go now?" I say. "There's a train in thirty minutes."

Today was going to be a good day for skating, I had decided. I had the feeling I could pull off any trick. Maybe even the five-stair. I'd done some good switch back-side flips with the soap in the basin that morning. The soap had flicked and tumbled accurately under my fingers.

QUESTION
What does Josh mean when he says, "I just came with the deal"?

"Today?" Mum says.

"Mum – I always skate on Sundays."

"I thought you knew we were doing family things today."

"Doing what? You didn't say."

"Helping Raymond get the potatoes in."

CHARACTER ANALYSIS

"If we act like a family and live like a family, we will be a family."

Do you think Mum's statement reflects a true picture of what makes a family? Why/why not?

"Mum."

"Josh." My mother narrows her eyes at me. I look away and glimpse the birthday cake on the counter.

"If he doesn't want to, he doesn't have to," says Raymond.

I LOOK AT HIM, READY TO SMILE. HE DOES UNDERSTAND.

"He can just go on taking us for granted. It's no different from any other day."

I press my lips together and look back out the window. My toes flip around in my socks, as if I'm doing a kick flip under the table.

"You can at least stack the dishwasher and wash up," Mum says.

"Okay." I push my chair back and take the plates out to the kitchen. I scrape the pans and wash them in hot, soapy water. I pull some good grinds in the plastic cups with the dishwashing brush.

Twenty minutes left to catch the train. I go up to my room for my board.

OPINION

Do you think the author has stereotyped step-family relationships? Why/why not?

I YELL...

"Goodbye, Mum!" and run down the steps to the path.

FREEDOM!

Raymond is standing in front of the garage, looking at the garden. I turn my head to look, too.

The vegetable garden is covered in long grass and a vigorous leafy weed. In the sun and light wind, the weeds and grass move slightly.

TIME TO GO.

But I hesitate to turn away. It's something about the way Raymond is standing. I remember Mum's words – how no one had made a fuss of Raymond much.

And when did he do that for me? I think.

Raymond just stands there. It reminds me of that hopeless feeling I had when I sat on the fence in the truck bay, not wanting to enter the skateboard competition.

I take a few steps towards him.

"I can help for fifteen minutes."

"No, don't bother," says Raymond.

"I want to," I say.

Raymond turns to look at me. "You ever planted potatoes before?"

"No. We just buy them."

"The thing about potatoes is, you put one in the ground and it gives you back ten. Out of the bounty of the soil."

"Like ten percent interest – oh no, it's ten times," I say.

LANGUAGE FEATURE

Analogy

What analogy did the author use here? How did it help your understanding? What message did the author want to convey to the reader?

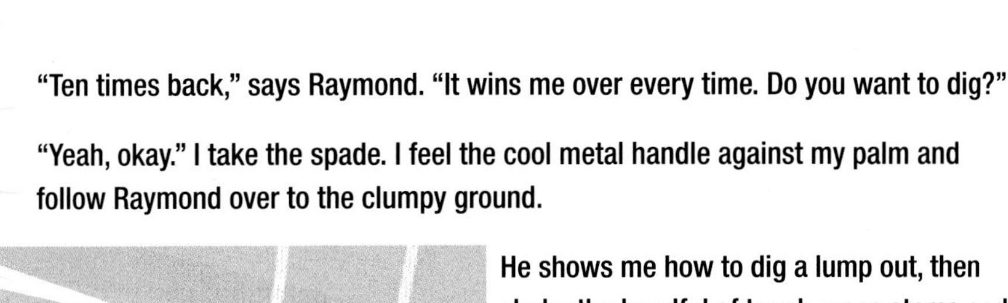

"Ten times back," says Raymond. "It wins me over every time. Do you want to dig?"

"Yeah, okay." I take the spade. I feel the cool metal handle against my palm and follow Raymond over to the clumpy ground.

He shows me how to dig a lump out, then shake the handful of tough grass stems and sappy weeds till the soil falls out. The pile of grass and weeds with their bare, thready roots grows bigger. The patch of garden that's clear and brown hardly seems to change. I wipe the sweat off my forehead with the back of my hand.

THE TRAIN WILL ALREADY HAVE LEFT BY NOW.

"We'll get one row of potatoes in, then I'll drive you to town," says Raymond.

"Okay," I say.

We set the potatoes out in a row in the crumbly soil. They already have tough green knobs of shoots, ready to burst into life.

"Don't knock them," Raymond says, "or they might not grow."

CHARACTER ANALYSIS

What inferences can you make about Josh from the way he responds to Raymond's hopelessness?

THE THING ABOUT POTATOES IS YOU PUT ONE IN THE GROUND AND IT GIVES YOU BACK TEN OUT OF THE BOUNTY OF THE SOIL

"Five potatoes instead of ten," I say.

"You've got it."

When we get to the skatepark, Raymond keeps the engine idling.

"Do you want to stay and watch me?" I ask.

"Things to do," says Raymond.

I take my board and get out of the car.

"Thanks for the help," says Raymond. I lift my hand as the car backs away.

QUESTION GENERATE

What questions can you ask about the role skateboarding has in Josh's life?

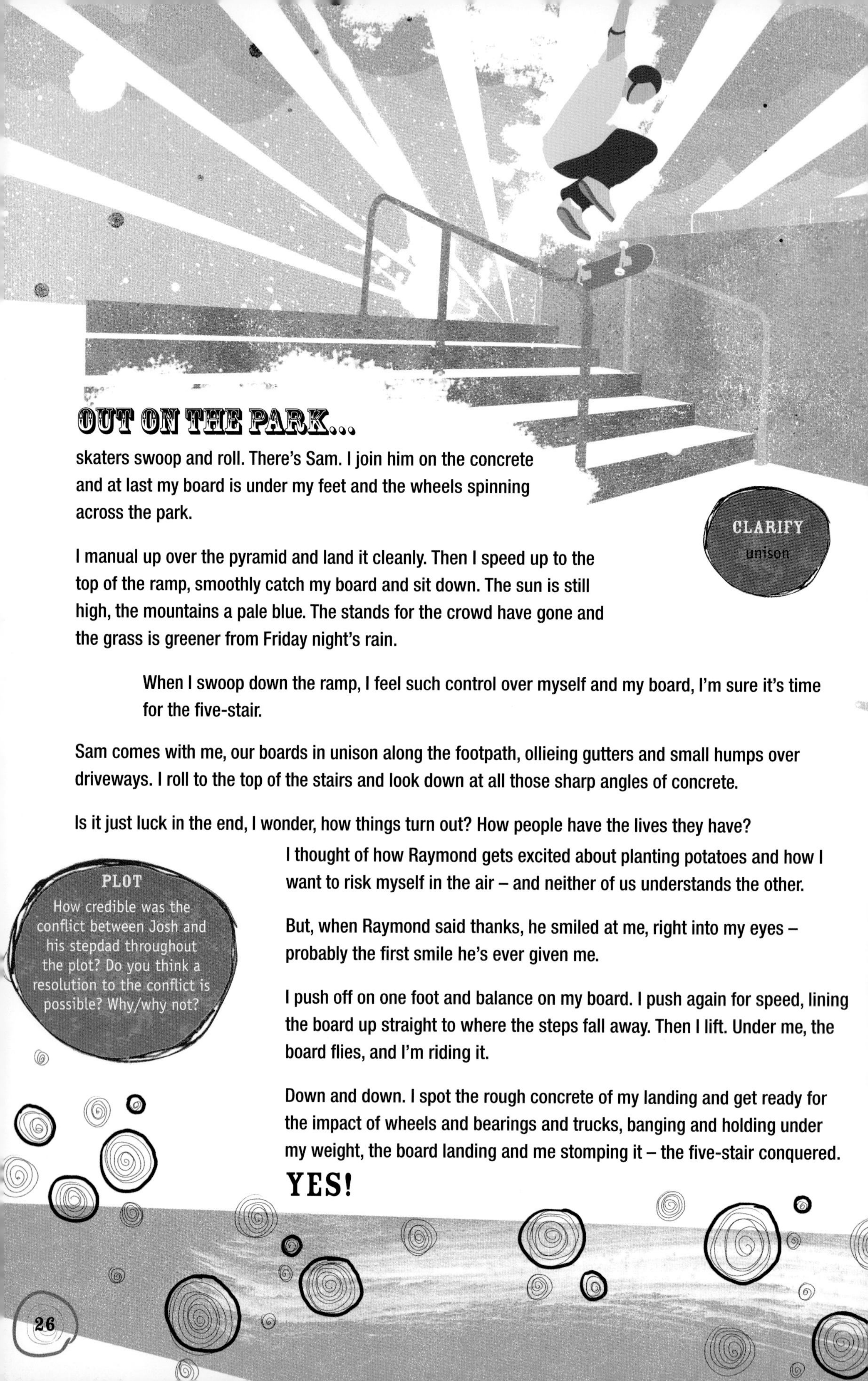

OUT ON THE PARK...

skaters swoop and roll. There's Sam. I join him on the concrete and at last my board is under my feet and the wheels spinning across the park.

CLARIFY
unison

I manual up over the pyramid and land it cleanly. Then I speed up to the top of the ramp, smoothly catch my board and sit down. The sun is still high, the mountains a pale blue. The stands for the crowd have gone and the grass is greener from Friday night's rain.

When I swoop down the ramp, I feel such control over myself and my board, I'm sure it's time for the five-stair.

Sam comes with me, our boards in unison along the footpath, ollieing gutters and small humps over driveways. I roll to the top of the stairs and look down at all those sharp angles of concrete.

Is it just luck in the end, I wonder, how things turn out? How people have the lives they have? I thought of how Raymond gets excited about planting potatoes and how I want to risk myself in the air – and neither of us understands the other.

PLOT
How credible was the conflict between Josh and his stepdad throughout the plot? Do you think a resolution to the conflict is possible? Why/why not?

But, when Raymond said thanks, he smiled at me, right into my eyes – probably the first smile he's ever given me.

I push off on one foot and balance on my board. I push again for speed, lining the board up straight to where the steps fall away. Then I lift. Under me, the board flies, and I'm riding it.

Down and down. I spot the rough concrete of my landing and get ready for the impact of wheels and bearings and trucks, banging and holding under my weight, the board landing and me stomping it – the five-stair conquered.

YES!

AUTHOR PURPOSE

What overall message did the author want to convey to the reader?

READING BETWEEN THE LINES

Josh acknowledges that lack of understanding has affected the relationship between his stepdad and himself. What effect do you think this will have on the relationship now?

THINK ABOUT THE TEXT

MAKING CONNECTIONS

What connections can you make to the characters, plot, setting and themes of **COOL GRINDS**?

TEXT TO SELF

- dealing with conflict in step-family relationships
- facing criticism and lack of understanding at home
- having a goal
- persevering to achieve something
- facing pre-contest nerves
- losing confidence in yourself
- being afraid of failure
- being self-focused
- seizing opportunity
- recognising that lack of understanding affects relationships

TEXT TO TEXT/MEDIA

Talk about texts/media you have read, listened to or seen that have similar themes and compare the treatment of theme and the differing author styles.

TEXT TO WORLD

Talk about situations in the world that might connect to elements in the story.

SHORT STORY

THINK ABOUT WHAT DEFINES A SHORT STORY

A short story is a brief fictional narrative that usually deals with only one or two main characters and a single plot.

THINK ABOUT THE PLOT

Decide on a plot that has an introduction, problems and a solution, and write them in the order of sequence.

Build your story to a turning point. This is the most exciting/suspenseful part of the story.

Decide on an event to draw the reader into your story. What will the main conflict/problem be?

Climax

Conflict

Falling Action

Decide on a final event that will bring your story to a close by:
- **resolving the conflict/problem**

or,
- **leave the conclusion open.**

Rising Action

Set the scene: who is the story about? When and where is it set?

Introduction

Resolution

Focus on one major event or conflict and avoid sub-plots. Introduce the conflict early on and limit the characters that the event affects.

Build your story to a turning point – the most exciting/suspenseful part of the story – quickly by limiting background information that slows down the action.

Conclude your short story by:
- resolving the conflict/problem or,
- leaving the conclusion open to the reader's imagination through an abrupt ending.

THINK ABOUT THE CHARACTERS

Explore:

- how they think, feel and act
  - what motivates their behaviour
    - their inner feelings.

Keep your characters in the spotlight and only show the reader as much of their background as is necessary for the plot.

DECIDE ON THE SETTING

ATMOSPHERE/ MOOD

LOCATION

TIME

WRITING A SHORT STORY

HAVE YOU...

- Included a short introduction that grabs the reader's interest?
- Introduced fewer main characters than longer stories?
- Written a simple and fast-moving plot?
- Avoided unnecessary details of setting/characters?
- Used adjectives with restraint?
- Written a story that can be read in one session (ie fewer than 10,000 words)?

...DON'T FORGET TO REVISIT YOUR WRITING.

DO YOU NEED TO CHANGE, ADD OR DELETE ANYTHING TO IMPROVE YOUR STORY?